I0721298

60 Years Return to the Battle of Bulge

To Remember Our Past as It Was

Frank W. Maresca

Zeta Publishing

Ocala, FL

Zeta Publishing, Inc
3850 SE 58th Ave
Ocala, FL 34480
www.zetapublishing.com

Ordering Information:
Quantity sales. Special discounts are available on quantity purchases by corporations, associations, and others. For details, contact the publisher at the address above.
Orders by U.S. trade bookstores and wholesalers. Please contact Zeta Publishing: Tel: (352) 694-2553; Fax: (352) 694-1791 or visit www.zetapublishing.com

ISBN: 978-1-947191-14-3 (sc)

ISBN: 978-1-947191-15-0 (e)

ISBN: 978-1-947191-38-9 (hc)

Library of Congress Control Number: 2017948820

Printed in the United States of America

Digital Photos taken during the 60th VBOB Celebration December 6th, just prior to our departure for the reception at the Belgium Embassy in WDC.

Note: numbers left out are due to the poor quality of the photos taken or were test photos, etc.

Frank Maresca

Test Photos.

Inside my room: number 379 at the Marriott on the campus of the University of Maryland.

Herb Ridyard, and his wife "Laura Bush" drop in unexpectedly at the Marriott. That's Gary Higgins a traveling buddy seated across from Herb's wife. The other gentleman is unknown.

Meeting General Van de Ven for the first time. That's Ambassador Van Daele of Belgium in the background.

Our arrival at the Belgium Embassy in WDC. The greeter in blue uniform is Brigadier General Van de Ven. Ambassador van Daele is just to his right.

Vets begin to mingle with honored guests of the Ambassador. The woman on the left is the Private Secretary to the Ambassador. That's the Ridyards in the center of the photo.

Jack Dederer who became a close comrade during the trip, is showing a WWII picture of a hunting lodge his unit occupied during WWII to Ambassador Deale.

The Ambassador's Social Secretary.

An honored guest of the Ambassador Mr. Richard Kurasiewicz, Sr.
International Analyst, NATO BRANCH.

Frank Maresca

Self-posing with Mr. Kurasiewicz.

Lobby of the Marriott.

Going through the
"Check Point" for
identification.

General Ven displays a sense of humor.

Part of the gang of 46 sits and waits for our plane.

One of the vets that went on the Airbus, and made up the AIRBUS
wing of our invasion of Belgium, and Luxembourg.

In the waiting room at Andrews Air Force Base just after a brief screening.
General Van de Ven is warning us about being without a certain coin that he has
just distributed to us. Caught without it meant a free beer for him.

On the Airbus waiting for it to take off. Note how empty it is. 46 doesn't take up any room!

Aboard the AIRBUS. It's about 2:45pm, and we are about to get underway.

We are seated on the bus looking at the Airbus minutes after landing in the rain at the Brussels airport, northeast of the city. It's about 3 am Belgian time as we wait to drive to our quarters in Brussels: The Belgium Royal Air force Academy.

Waiting at the Belgium Air Force Academy for chow.
The General is already starting to joke around.

We begin to eat. I'm at the far right.

Eating in the mess hall of the Belgium Air Force Academy on our first morning in Brussels, Belgium. That is General Van de Ven looking over the itinerary for the day.

We gather outside after breakfast. Waiting for our tour bus.

We begin gathering outside the lobby of the Academy to board the Belgian Air Force bus which will take us to our first tour point. It is about 8 am. The buildings across from us are part of the Belgium Air Force Academy.

The entrance to the Palace court yard. It was once used by the visitors coming by carriage.

Assembled at the foot of one of the grand staircases to meet, and greet General Guido Mertens, Chief of the King's Household. That's Bob Rhodes the official Photographer at the foot of the steps. Our Guide Martene, who happens to be the King's personal secretary, is standing to the right of the two generals, and our Tour Coordinator, Earl Hart.

We begin to move through the King's household. In the addition to me in front, that tall lovely lady is Martene, the King's Personal Secretary.

Ballroom with massive chandeliers, lit for a special occasion: US.

The balcony area near the ceiling is where the orchestra sits to play when a ball is held.

This room we are told serves as a gust reception room.

The room with the assembled plush red chairs, and red carpeted dais is the room where the King received dignitaries, diplomats, and other notables.

A room whose special significance we are told, lies with two tablets of the Ten Commandments sculptured by a Belgian artist at the behest of one of the early kings. They occupy a space above a grand doorway.

The Christian symbol for Christmas was being set up while we were there.

Martene identified this room with its green ceiling, and African motif as the Congo Room.
It was added to the palace to signify Belgium as being an empire country. Today it signifies
Belgium's close tie with its former colony in Africa.

The entire group of 46 gather together on a staircase for a Group Photo. The last photo shows us leaving for our next stop.

Leaving the palace via its cobbled stone courtyard.

A tower on top of an imposing building across from the palace.

Another entrance way into the palace. This is a rear entrance. The palace is situated on an imposing square, part of which is caught in photos 26 to 29 that follow.

A very impressive building with its many balconies.

Other edifices that graced the square behind the palace.

The General told us a tale about some of the statues that crown the buildings. In 29 one of the three ladies is pregnant. One is point at a mounted figure nearby as the culprit. He denies the charge, and points at a figure across the square as the one. Same says not him, pointing at a figure atop of a corner building in 29, who happens to be the Bishop. Said same appears to be looking down sheepishly.

                    Frank Maresca

The continuation of The General's tale about the location of the figures in question.

Reception at Hotel de Ville (City Hall) of Brussels.
This is one of the long decorated halls in the Ville.

Jack Dederer and Jack McAuliffe. They looked so much a like that I kept getting confused as to who was who. So, to remedy the situation I made them brothers, and each time that I saw them, I would ask one or the other, "Where is your brother?"

Frank Maresca

The Councill 1 Room where the deputies meet with the Mayor.

Entering the church of the Madonna with Tears.

The "Wedding Room". Whenever a couple wanted to get married in City Hall, they requested such a favor. The Mayor officiated at the ceremony. The couples brought their own champagne, and glasses, to be sat down on one of the assigned tables. After the wedding ceremony, the wedded couples gathered in the Wedding Room for a celebration. The mayor usually joins them in a toast.

A decorated ceiling in this ancient Ville.

Although dark, this room contained some very large paintings of the succession of kings of Belgium. In addition, it is used as the official room for meeting dignitaries, and special visitors to City Hall.

Meeting the Mayor of Brussels.

The Mayor greets us with a short speech, and we toast one another in champagne.

Our Military Police escort viewed through the windshield of our bus. These men were with us through most of our time in Belgium. Here we are on our way to Belgium's most beautiful city: Burges.

                     Frank Maresca

The Catholic Church of the Madonna with Tears in Burges.

Another view of the sacred statute of thee Madonna.

View of the rear of the church.

The very ornate pulpit in the Church of the Madonna with Tears.

A photo shop through a side window of the bus of a comrade, and a view of the entrance to Burges's Fish Market.

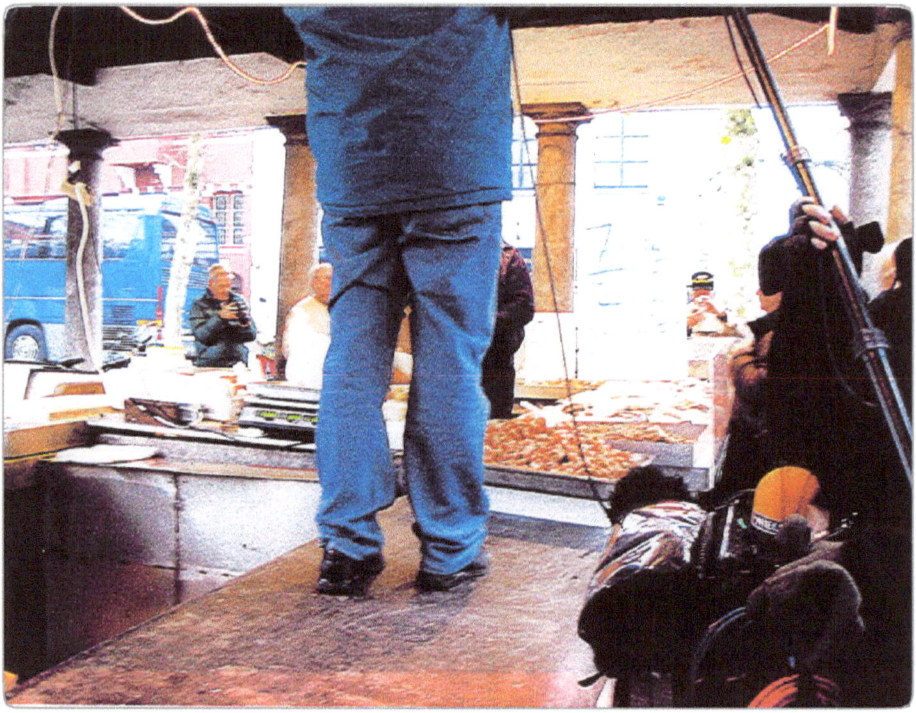

Lobster! Shrimp! Cod anyone?

More of the same in quantity. There was a fish fry going on, and the aroma has us salivating.

Boarding the tour boats at Burges.

The canals that made Burges famous, and beautiful. One of the motorboats that we took to tour a portion of Burges's canal system on a gray, overcast, and bitterly cold day.

A portion of Burges's main square.

Another view showing the city's Ville, and part of the famous House of Burges.

The very ornate House of Burges.

We stop at the Ville of the Mayor to warm ourselves with Orange Juice, etc, etc.

The photo of Her Majesty, the Queen of Belgium in the Reception Room of the Hotel de Ville of Burges. This reception was a surprise as it was not listed on our schedule. It was most welcomed as it got us out of the cold. We drank wine and champagne as well!

The Mayor bending elbows with us as we share in his generosity and welcome.

One of the great rooms in the Burges Ville decorated in gold leaf.
This room served as a reception room.

Another room similar in design, and decorated in gold leaf.
It appears to have the same purpose as the first.

Waiting to be served lunch at the Navy Barracks at St. Kruis in Burges.

Having a conversation while waiting for lunch as prepared by trainees at the School for Cooks and Services at St. Kruis.

We gather outside of the World War Cemetery at Ypres. Belgium for a prepping.

Cooks and Waiters lined up to receive our applause for a fine meal well served.

The World War 1 Cemetery of the honored dead, mostly British, outside of Ypres, Belgium. It was a cloudy, foggy and misty afternoon as we walked amongst some of the tens of thousands of graves there. Many were decorated with poppies.

The main portion of the semi-circular archway. It appeared to have been built to give a visitor the feeling that it was there to both protect and embrace the dead that lay before it.

A view looking towards the left which gives an idea of the great size of the cemetery. An equal portion stretched to the right of where we were standing.

The main Arch raised to honor those who were killed before Ypres. All the walls are covered with hundreds of names.

A sort of altar upon which wreaths formed from poppies were laid out row upon row.

A shot to show some of the columns with names etched on the walls of the Arch at Ypres.

The incongruity of it all! Nearly surrounded by a WWI battlefield where they continue to find remains of the dead, and a cemetery that abuts along its boundaries. Ypres decorated with lights of Christmas appears ready to celebrate the holidays.

St. George Church erected by the British after WWI to honor the various units of the British Expeditionary Force that fought for Ypres, and were decimated during the battle.

Part of the walls inside the church which are covered with large shiny brass plaques in memory of fallen comrades.

We quaff a few beers before dinner at Iper Barracks.

Every chair in the church was covered with a seat cushion bearing the coat of arms or insignia of a unit of the BEF that fought in and around Ypres.

Waiting for dinner at Iper Barracks, a Belgian Army Camp. What better way to kill time before dinner than to quaff a few beer with comrades?

The "suds" keep flowing to quench the thirst of men wondering, "What's for dinner?".

Two comrades content to sit loose and drink slow.

This is the walkway into Fort Brendonk.

Dinner is served at Iper Barracks.

The visit to Fort Brendonk begins. There were two German concentration camps in Belgium. This was one of them. The sign is a warning in German, Dutch, and French. Its literal translation is "Halt! On your way! This Gate is closed!".

In a small museum just inside the gate. The Curator/Manager of the Fort is greeting us and welcoming us to the site.

The Mayor (note: he wears a yellow sash as a badge or mark of his authority) is reading a prepared speech which he delivered in two languages: English and French.

On the walk to the main entrance to the Fort. The top of the entrance way served as the basis for mounting guns to defend Brussels and Liege from the Germans during WWI and WWII.

Our guide is explaining the patch worn by men conscripted in the German Army like those in
the photos behind him.

The altar with the Nazi symbol and three votive lights were for Germans who died while in
service at the Fort/Concentration Camp.

One of the many areas in the camp where the prisoners worked; in the open regardless of the
weather; with little food; often with no chance to relive themselves; working with crude tools
to move tons of dirt to reshape the camp's outer walls.

Enlarged photo of captured Belgian soldiers. All but one were worked to death. The survivor is the man in yellow. He lived to write a book about camp life.

One of many corridors containing tiny eight men cells.

A better view of both the corridor(s) and cells. A small blue cape hangs on the wall at the end of the corridor. It was used to tie around a prisoner's head so he couldn't see who was flogging him. The Germans used prisoners from other cell areas to administer the punishment under penalty of death.

The revised wall with fortified base for supporting heavy gun emplacements. Tour members strolling by.

Earthen walls erected by forced labor.
One of the watch towers is in the background.

More fortified gun emplacements.

Posts near a portion of earthen wall used by firing squads to shoot those who tried to escape, etc.

Corner area where the Germans hung prisoners.

A moat that ran part way around the Fort. A boxcar stands alone across the moat. It's all that remains of a boxcar train that was used by the Germans to transport Jews to "The East" (Auschwitz).

Having luch at Airbase 1 Tactical Wing at Beauvechain, Belgium.

Entrance to the mess hall at the Tactical Wing. The insignia of a jet fighter signifies that this place is a fighter base.

The people who command the base. The three civilians are in charge of both administrative affairs, and the air museum that is housed on the base. The officer is the Commandant, a full bird (Colonel). He hosted the lunch for us.

Fresh air part of the air museum. The planes are retired fighters.

The second wave of VBOB members making the 60th Tour arrive from the States, and are warmly greeted by the members that came over on the Airbus.

Bill Leopold of the Leigh Valley Chapter, Pa., getting familiar with the Academy's mess hall.

Other members of the Leigh Valley Chapter, fresh from the States, taking a coffee break. They re Judy Greenhalgh VP, Leigh Valley Chapter of the VBOB, and Phllis, and Bill Leopold.

Royal Military Museum in Brussels, Facade of the museum is shaped in the horseshoe fashion. An impressive arch connects the two wings of the facade. The same was used in designing the WWI Cemetery entrance at Ypres.

Photo shots showing parts of the wings of the facade of the museum and its entrance arch.

The right wing of the Museum's facade.

Jack Dederer posing before a Sherman tank at the entrance of the museum.

If he can do it, so can I!

WWII V1 Rocket. It was better known to all of us at the "Buss Bomb". Same is seen suspended from the vaulted led ceiling of the museum.

Part of our group sitting in for an orientation on the museum.

Self with friend before an earlier version of Germany's Tiger Tank.

A WWI Triplane used by the Germans during the great war. This was the "Red Baron's" trademark plane that he flew most of his fighter missions.

The Tank invented by the British and was first used in WWI, sits in the corner to remind one and all of the horrors that the combatants of WWI had to face during hand to hand combat.

A French 75 mounted on a special ramp to enable its crew to fire up at planes. It was the forerunner of the anti-aircraft weapons used in WWII.

"On the road again", with military escort, we head for our hotel in Houffalize, Beglium.

At the Hotel OL FOSSE D'OUTH.
A brief gathering of friends.

Through a window dimly we get our first glimpse of our hotel: OL FOSSE D'OUTH.
It's a mountainside resort.

In the lobby of the hotel waiting for room assignments and the reunion with one's luggage.

One of the best things that happened on the tour; the meeting and bonding with a great bunch of guys. We were a real team full of fun and adventurous spirits.

We have ate, drunk heart, and are happy!

The Marriott's. One of the few times that we saw Ennio's wife not busy taking pictures.

The actual field where the Malmedy massacre occurred. Part of a roadway
appears in the left lower corner. The German SS trucks and wewapon carriers
lined up on this road with thier machine guns facing towards the field where the
Americans massed.

This wooden framed building was where 5 wounded American survivors of the massacre crawled to, to wait for the Germans to leave the area before seeking help from nearby American units. Today it serves as a restaurant. Master Sergeant Tom Dobinski, Armore, and with whom I toured the area told me that today's owners are German sympathizers and therefore, not very friendly.

Awaiting lunch at Camp Elsenborn.

Yours truly! Waiting lunch
at Camp Elsenborn.

After lunch, we began gathering outside the camp's messing facilities.

Jack Dederer posing to show the happy face that goes with a full belly.

Jack's shot of me on a side road in the camp.
Note the white frost on the ground. It was cold!!!

To check my camera's functioning in the cold, I took this picture of a comrade.

Shots taken through a side window of our bus.
We are on the road leading out of the camp.

A view of the interior of our bus.

A shot worth forgetting.

Ligneuville where we stopped to pay homage to 8 GIs of the 9th Armored Division who were murdered by the SS. The area before the red buildings contains the ruins of an 11th century abbey.

A shot o f Main Street in Ligneuville.

Diorama of a field medical crew attending to the wounded just in back of the front lines.

A restored WWII Jeep. This one reminded me of the one that evacuated me when I was wounded. They threw me on top of the hood, face down, and told me to hold on for dear life. I remember grabbing the windshield with my left hand and part of the fender with my right all the while begging Hurley our 1st Sergeant to hold on to me by my pants belt as he stood up in the jeep.

Another view of Ligneuville's Main Street.

A grand arch with a beautiful stained glass window. Some said that the arch was a
memorial to the fallen of WWI.

A veteran (the bearded one) who knew some of the murdered men and his traveling companion.

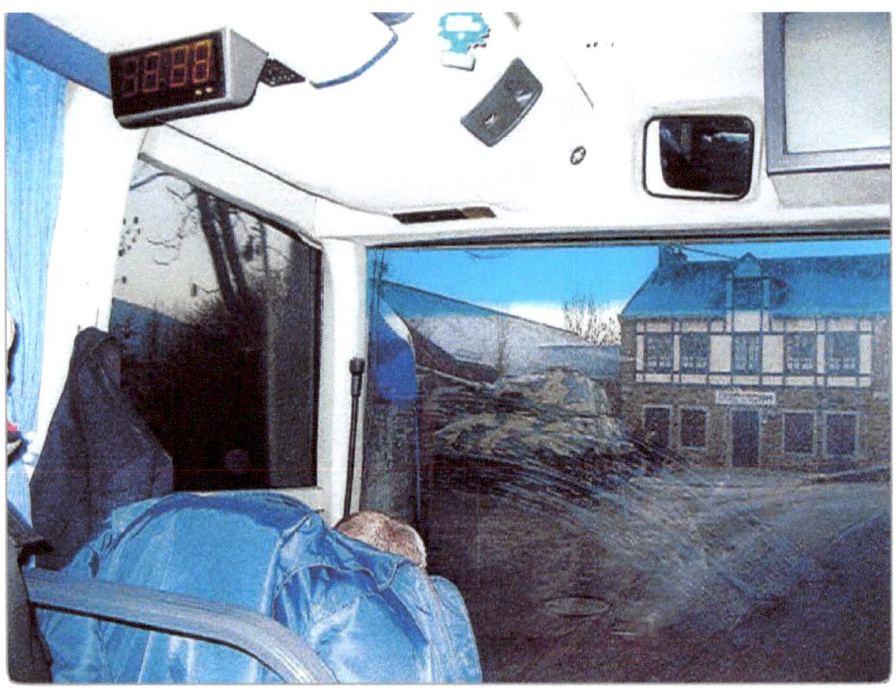

LaGleize's Tiget Tank viewed through a window of a our bus.

Another view through a window.

The monster itself! It struck fear in us once! It struck a cord of respect for it now!

Members of the Leheigh Chapter of VBOB.

Members of the Leigh Valley Chapter of the VBOB together at the La Gleize Museum:
Bill Leopold? Herb Ridyard, and me.

A second shot of the gang from the Leigh Valley Chapter. I am manning the camera. They
are The Leopold, Bill, and Phyllis, Mr. Unknown, and the Ridyards.
The Museum is in the background.

Bill provides his autograph.

A foggy day as viewed through the bus's windshield. We are heading for Echternachl Luxembourug to see the General Patton Memorial Museum.

The entrance to the General Patton Memorial Museum.

Diorama of a CP at the front, one of many dioramas that could be seen inside the museum.

For some strange reason, I took a photo of old "Blood and Guts", sideways.

Diorama of seriously wounded about to be loaded into an ambulance (the Meat Wagon).

This photo speaks for itself. It shows all how much we loved Uncle Adolf!

Photo was taken to show two items that we saw our elders using during our growing up years: a can of Half n Half pipe tobacco and Lucky Strikes cigarettes. The green color of Lucky Strikes disappeared at the beginning of the war. I remember a disk jockey by the name of Martin Block saying "Lucky Strike green has gone to war".

152a looking over war items of great interest to me.

This shot shows shelves jammed with all types of field rations used during the war. Many were issued to us to keep mind and body together during those deep freeze days of the Bulge.

A shot of what those who erected this diorama thought we wore during the Bulge days. I looked like the one to the right with modifications.

German equipment and mobile tank Destroyer in the background.

Alleyway in back of the Museum with a parked Sherman. Tank at the end of the alley.

Making our way through Ettle bruck on our way to Diekirch, their museum, and lunch.

Getting ready to eat at the Cultural Centre of Diekirch "AAl SEEREI".

Waiting for lunch to be served and wondering what kind of soup we were going to get. The soup that we got was not the ever familiar green soup that we had come to expect whenever soup was mentioned as an entry to a Belgian dinner. It looked and tasted to our joy like real vegetable soup!

I catch Judy Greenhalgh our Chapter VP, and Bob Rhodes, our roving Photographer in a picture taking mode.

In the old days of Army life, it was called "Chowing Down".

Clay Christensen along with a few others admiring the structural work of the Culture's mess hall. Turns out that the building was once part of the lumber mill.

10th Century castle overlooking Germany, the Saauer River,

...and Vianden. A low cover of fog and mist blanked the area, including a portion of the
Siegfried Line.

 Frank Maresca

Vianden in the valley and within the shadows of the castle and Germany's Siegfried Line.

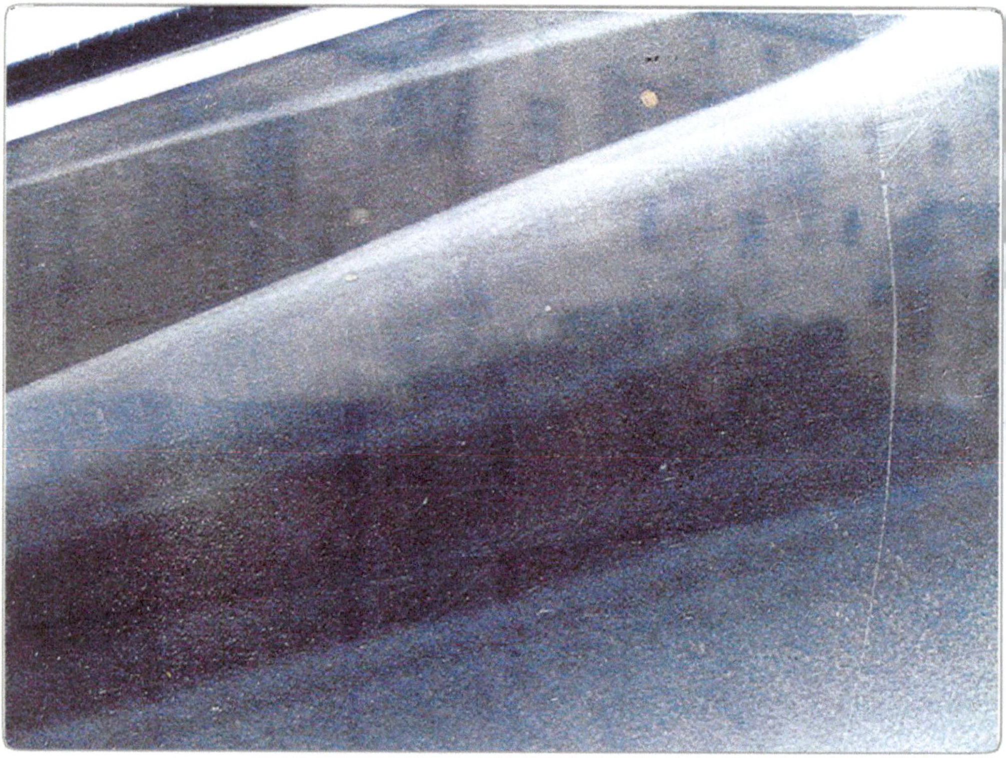

Another one of those photo shots worth forgetting!

Face to face with a strong point on the Siegfried Line. It was a bit o f a surprise that you could move back and forth over borders, in this case, Luxembourg and Germany without being challenged.

"Ace" Parker, former President of the 75th Division Association posing in front of a banker complex in the Siegfried Line.

A roadway that leads through iron gates into Germany.

Judy and I pose before a bunker complex. Same had a large size artillery or tank shell hole. We hid it by our pose. However, it can be seen in photo #106.

Standing outside the residence of the US Ambassador to Lexumbourg, Ambassador Terpeluk. We are to meet and pose with the Ambassador, one on one. Champagne, win and the ever ubiquitous orange juice along with hors d'oeuvres await us.

COZ (Cozzolino O'Neil) poses for a shot in the warm and snug residence.

Ambassador Terpeluk. Each of us were photographed with the Ambassador and were given a couple of minutes to talk to him. Since he was from Boston, I told him of a fan that held up a sign in the form of a tombstone during the Division Series. It read: "Win a World Series before I pass away". He got a real kick out of it.

We gather to hear a welcome talk by the Ambassador.

Family photos and photos showing visits by Presidents Clinton, Bush, and several notables.

An oil painting of General Patton which occupies an almost shrine
like place in the Ambassador's residence.

The distaff half of the Ambassador's team. Mrs. Terpeluk who was warm and gracious to me, and all, and posed readily when asked. Here she is talking to two of my cohorts, one of which is our Chapter VP: Judy Greenhalgh.

The Ambassadress posing with one of the Army Nurses who served with us during WWII.

I haven't the foggiest why I took this photo! Maybe I wanted to show that we provide roofs over the heads of those who also serve. Who knows!

The Ambassadress and I in a snug hold.

Clervaux, Luxembourg. We arrive to begin a walk through a shopping district on our way to take part in the CEBA G.I. Statute Ceremony.

We walk up a narrow shopping street passing quaint stores like Liquor/win stores, Confectionery stores, Bakery shops, restaurants, coffee shops, etc.

As we progress, the street takes on a pedestrian appearance, with street designs, multi colored brick connoting walking paths, etc.

More shops and the local hotel.

We arrived at the ceremonial spot: The G.I. Statute.

The place was small. Yet, over 230 of us along with the Navy Band, dignitaries, TV Media and citizens jammed into the area, even occupying windows, and balconies. The one touching thing that caught my eye was several fathers holding up their offspring in the windows to see the not to be forgotten ceremony.

The Navy Band arrived playing a stirring match.

The display of the colors of two countries: Luxembourg and the United States.

One of the members of the Honor Guard collapsed from standing at ridged attention thereby impeding his circulation.

Back in the town square waiting for the buses to take us to our next stop.

While waiting, I panned camera so as to take some shots of what was on the high ground around Clervaux. Modest apartments rung part of the town square.

Part of a well-reserved castle situated behind a high wall towered over some business buildings, and apartment houses.

We are bussed to the Clervaux Community Center. There we view some Battle of the
Bulge memorabilia. For example: a recently dug up jeep that had hit a land mine in a skirmish
near Clervaux during the early days of the German offensive.

Part of the trapping that go with celebrating: row upon row of champagne glasses.

Boxes of C and D rations stacked before a diorama of a...

German Red Cross station. Note that the D rations were made by the Cracker Jack Co.

A better view of the diorama with cases of ammo lined before it.

Welcome address by the Mayor of Clervaux, Mr. Francis Stephany. Like all addresses and speeches that we heard, they were delivered in two languages: English and French.

The second speaker to address us was Mr. Camille Kohn, President of CEBA.

Mr. Khon was followed by the Under Secretary for the Navy.

I received Luxembourg's 60th Anniversary Medallion.

We are treated to a special luncheon courtesy of the Luxembourg Government. We are waiting for our servers to bring us soup. It was vegetable soup and it turned out to be very good soup! It was a far cry from the constant green soup that we got with Belgian fare.

Clervaux Community Center where we ate a good lunch.

Self in a Luxembourg Army jeep outside the Community Center where we just had lunch.

Jack Dederer and myself were fascinated by the size and utility of this vehicle. It was a two-seater, and appeared to be great for tooling around a city.

We just finished a farewell dinner at OL FOSSE d'OUTH hotel.

Farewell dinner at the OL Fosse d' Outh Hotel. We were given a game dinner consisting of Ostrich and Kagaroo meat with side vegetables. I drank the wine and ate the vegetables. Seated around the table were Cozzolino ONiel in red, Dwight Rist opposite Cozz and Bob Cook.

At another table facing the camera:Bill Leopold with wife Phyllis to his left.

t Luxembourg's National Bulge Memorial at Schumann's Eck in Wiltz, Luxembourg. I tried to get a picture of the Memorial's Plaque but two comrades, Earle Hart for one got in the way.

The second try was a success. That's Al Sussman in the trench coat in the background.

The Maryland contingent of the VBOB wanted one and all to know that they were there too.

The Grand Duchess of Luxembourg (the lady with the black hat), and mother of the two songs, Princes of Luxembourg arrived surrounded by VBOB veterans who were unaware of her status.

The Navy Band played a stirring march just prior to the beginning of ceremonies. Of note: it was cold!!

Another shot of that Maryland bunch this time showing such "notables" as Bill, and Phyllis Leopold, Jack Dederer's "brother" (Jack McAuliffe), and one of the two Army Nurses that were with us 60 years ago.

Posed in front of the plaque were Earle Hart, Trip Coordinator. Standing to the right of Earle were Christanne D'Haese, Tour Committee Coordinator with the Heir Apparent Duchess of Luxembourg.

The Princes of Luxembourg.

The Princes, along with the rest of us listened to the speeches made during the ceremony.

The Assistant Secretary for the US Airforce addressed one and all.

The laying of wreaths at the base of the Memorial. I believe the two Princes laid the wreaths with the current Grand Duchess (black hat) looking on.

The Princes being interviewed by members of the TV media.

Ceremony at the Mardasson Memorial in Bastogne. We were seated in the covered stands, called by the Belgians. The Tribune, opposite the steps to the Memorial.

Civilians along with the TV Media milled around.

The colors of all the cantons that make up the country of Belgium were displayed.
Civilians took up places along the top o f the steps of the Memorial and on top of the
Memorial itself.

The Navy Band up from its station in Spain entered the area playing a stirring march.
TV Cameramen and crowds were everywhere.

A contingent of Belgian soldiers marched in to take part in the ceremonies.

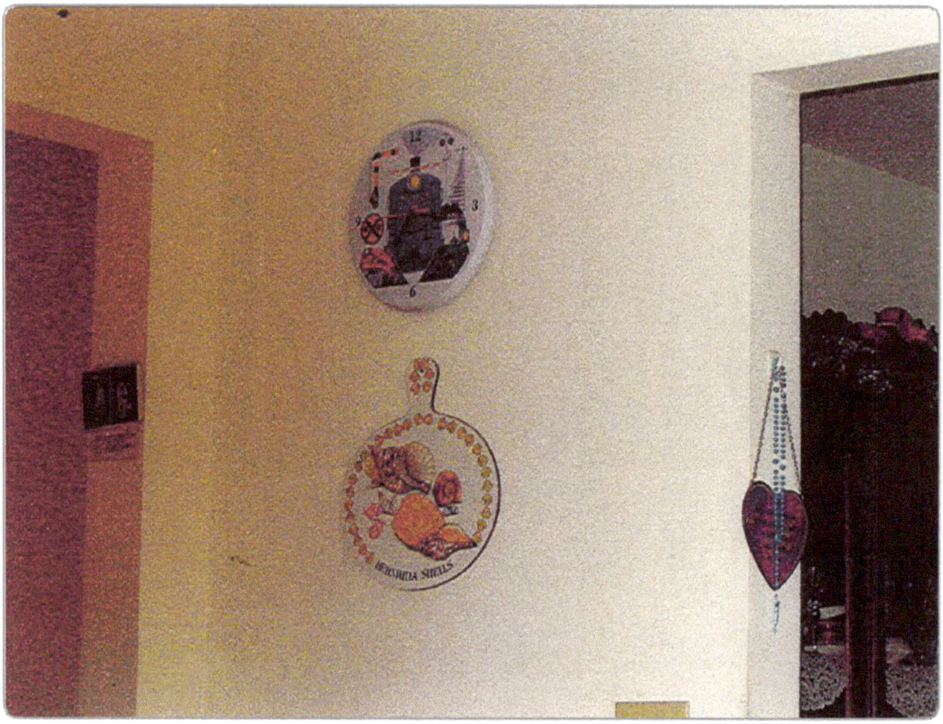

Test Photo

The Navy Band while playing a march takes it position alongside the colors preparatory to the planned ceremony.

The Mayor of Bastogne delivered the key address in English and then in French.

The playing of the National Anthems of the United States and Belgium. The Navy Band did the honors.

The Belgian contingent marched by to music supplied by the Navy Band.

251 View through front window of bus. Military Police on motorcycle leading the way. Street wet from gentle falling rain. Going the wrong way up a street in Bastogne.

Stopped at a community center for lunch. Small place.

Photo shows two lines. One: the lineup for the latrine. The other lined up beside the "the call of nature" ...the chow line. Fare served consisted of a sausage sandwich and either beer or coffee. Waiting for his care giver (Phyllis) to come with the viddels.

Unloading from our bus, and heading for the main gate...

...of the Luxembourg American Military Cemetery at Hamm. Heard of the foggy
day in London? We had one tool hurrying pass the Chapel Tower, its head scraping
against the lowering foggy' misty blanket which eventually embraced us all.

Another view of the Chapel Tower of Hamm.

We are given seats with warm cozy blankets. Many of us were tempted to roll
them up, and take them with us. The West Pylon which appears in the background,
displays relief map showing military operations in Western Europe.

Seated at the Chapel Tower at the American Military Cemetery at Hamm.

The way Jack Dederer has wrapped that blanket around...

...him gives an idea of what it was like to sit in the foggy mist waiting for proceedings to begin. Another view of the Chapel Tower. We are seated in front of its bronze doors. It was a miserable day!

Draped in blue blankets to keep us warm, and dry.

A shot of the West Pylon, and the three rows of seat set aside for guests. Note the folded blanket on each seat. An aside, I thought we were the honored guests!

Self seated beside Jack, and the other Blue clads. Note the resigned expression on our faces.

A moment of laughter at Hamm.

Posing for the camera. Soooo... Smile! "You're on candid Camera"!!

Some of the honored guests arrived. That's Speaker of the House of the United States Dennis Hastert standing in a black coat, and his gray head bare to the elements. The gentlemen with the black hat is a Congressman from North Dakota. The standee to his left is a Senator.

Huddled, and covered we listen to speeches delivered in two languages.

Wreaths which were presented by His Royal Highness the Grand Duke
of Luxembourg, and by the Veterans of the VBOB.

Ambassador Terpeluk, Ambassador to Luxembourg suggested that
a USO canteen-type evening be created for us.

Therefore, a 3 hours USO STYLED CANTEEN NIGHT was held at a Air Force
Stealth Bomber-Luxembourg facility in Dudelange, Luxembourg.

Inside a large airplane hanger, VBOB verterans, and some 300 plus gathered to have a good time. The Navy Band supplied the Big Band music of our time. Beer flowed like water. The cooks(?) made a stab at making hamburgers by frying them in deep boiling oil. They were big, flat, greasy, and didn't taste like hamburgers. They gave out great toll house cookies, and apple pie., however. A troupe imitating the Andrew Sisters, and dressed in red, white, and blue wowed us, and all with their renditions of old favorites.

A shot of a very small RC Church taken through the window of our bus. We are heading towards a special ceremony in Houffalize to honor the civilians who helped us during the fighting in the Bulge, and who died in many cases as the result of their help.

An area prepared for the ceremony.

The Navy Band gathered before the Junction Memorial Monument in Houffalize. Beside the monument it is the church that we will enter to hear a homily, and received a blessing.

Seated inside the church. We were escorted into the church by children of the town carrying little flags of the US, and Belgium.

We filed out of the church to a stirring applause by the town folk.

Outside before the Memorial Monument. We stand across from it surrounded by the children of the town.

In the church of Houffalize. The people before the special ceremony.

The children arranged before the special veterans.

Event over, we move out to the next event.

Ceremonies in progress. Photo shows
the heads of the small children.
Heading for the town's Community Center to receive a certificate.
We are following a contingent of Belgian soldiers.

A sober moment for we four.

Special guests who were invited to join with the vets too.

Some Chamber music to entertain us.

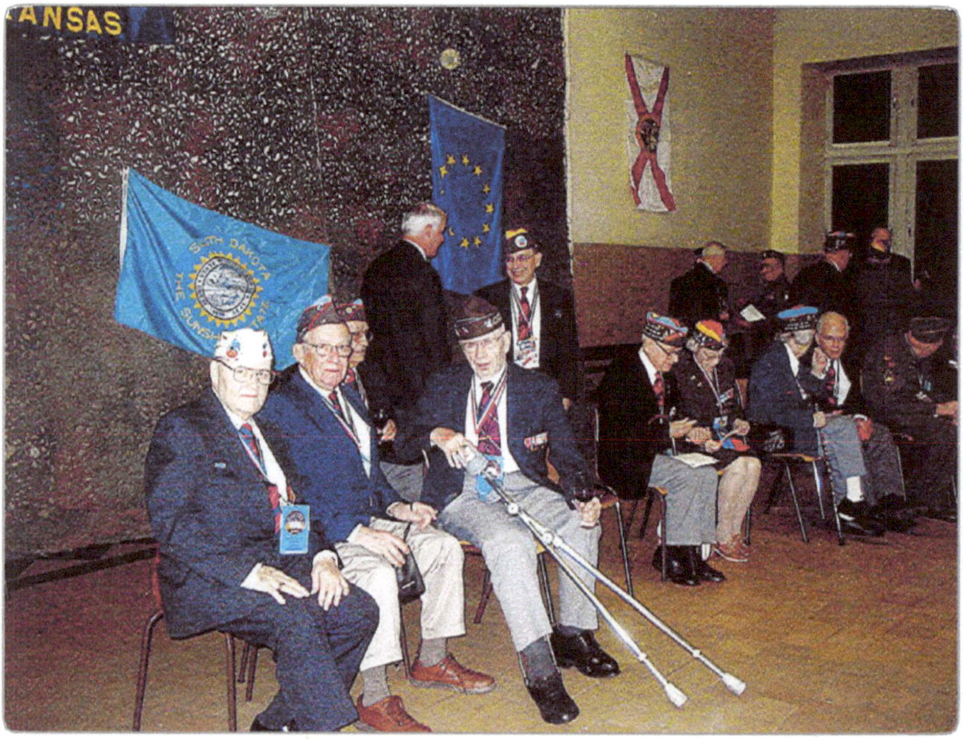

By now we are getting weary of waiting.

The moment when the Duke arrived. Media Cameramen were everywhere.

For a while, I thought that we were going to be pushed aside so that the special guests could meet and greet the Duke.

Moving up to meet and greet the Duke of Luxembourg.

He is about to make his entrance.

Himself: HRH Duke of Luxembourg.

HRH begins going down the line of vets drawn up to greet, shake his hands, and exchange few words.

Greeting Him is a former school teacher, VP of our chapter, and niece of an uncle who was kill in Luxembourg... Judie Greenhalgh. I am next in line to meet the Duke.

At Merceny place to watch the unfolding of the standard and the flag.

Merceny Place in Bastogne where they unfolded the standards and flags.

Honor Guard Participate in the pageantry of "Salute to the flag", and dipping of the colors.

Two comrades that begin the tour with me in WDC: Alfonso Sussmen and Cozzolino O'Neil.

We march up the streets to the McAuliffe Monument. That's Jack Dederer bringing up the rear on the right side.

Along the march, I meet the granddaughter of General Patton, Hellen Patton Plusczyk who very graciously stop to pose for me.

We arrive at McAuliffie Place where the ceremony is to take place. Note the detachment of Belgian soldiers standing at attention.

Shots of the crowd gathered to see the ceremony.

Providing an autograph of self.

Shots of the vets ringing the McAuliffie Monument. That's a Sherman Tank of the 4th Armored in the background.

Presentation of flowers and wreaths by the various organizations participating in the event.
A Naval Officer stands near the tank in the background crowd. During the USO night I met him
and his lovely wife while we were in a serving line. I addressed him as a Captain.

His wife exploded into laughter and she politely corrected me by saying that he was a full Admiral and Commander of Naval Forces in Europe as well as a Commander of Joint Force Command Naples. Red faced, I sputtered an apology. He would have none of it and gave me a beautiful medallion of his authority. His wife still laughing hugged me and he shook my hand warmly.

The ceremony is over. The rain starts to fall. The crowd begins to disperse. Photos were taken from the bus.

The crowd stops to wave farewell to us as we leave and we wave back!

A picture worth the effort to be forgotten.

A post war diner. For a moment, looking at this all aluminum dinner,
we thought we were back at the states.

A fleshpot cafe. A live bar, hot music, and nude dancers.
Yep! They got them too!

A plaque in honor of first American Nurse to be killed during the Bulge. The plaque marks the spot where she died.

We begin bus-tour-ride of the perimeter of the battle ground around the Bastogne. In view: a forested area where the Germans set up their tanks, and artillery pieces.

A road leading to a hotly contested point.

A crossroad where the Americans took a mauling but held their position.

Passing through a section of Bastogne we saw the lineup of war time vehicles (some 300) getting ready for the Big Show celebrating the entire combat moment, and break through rescue of the American defenders by the 4th Armored of the US.

New Car Dealer occupies the area where some bloody fighting took place.

Monument to civilian dead who were caught between the two forces.

Another hot spot fought over during the war.

Making our way through some heavy tourist-local folk traffic.

Jack Dederer, and myself pose with a representative of an Executive Staff. His rank: Secretariat.

A revisit to Mardasson Memorial. This time we are to be joined by his Royal Majesty the king o
Begium. It is at this point that we are separated from our companions. The reason is cloudy.

We sit amongst guests, and civilian in the stands directly across from the memorial. These stand
are called the Tribune. Colored banners are scattered throughout the crowd where the King will
enter.

The colors, and the ever growing crowd. The TV Media arrives in droves.

Another view of the people massing for the event.

Waiting for the arrival of the troops, and the Navy Band.

US Army marches in followed by the Navy Band.

Waiting for the arrival of his Majesty the King of Belgium.

He has arrived! We rise out of respect, the military snaps to attention.

The king in a tan overcoat is respectfully directed to the area before the Memorial where the ceremonies of the presentation are to begin.

He received a warm, and sustained applause.

He breaks the standing rule by going over to one end of the Tribune to shake hands with some of the vets, and guests that are assembled there.

He returns to the appointed place for him.

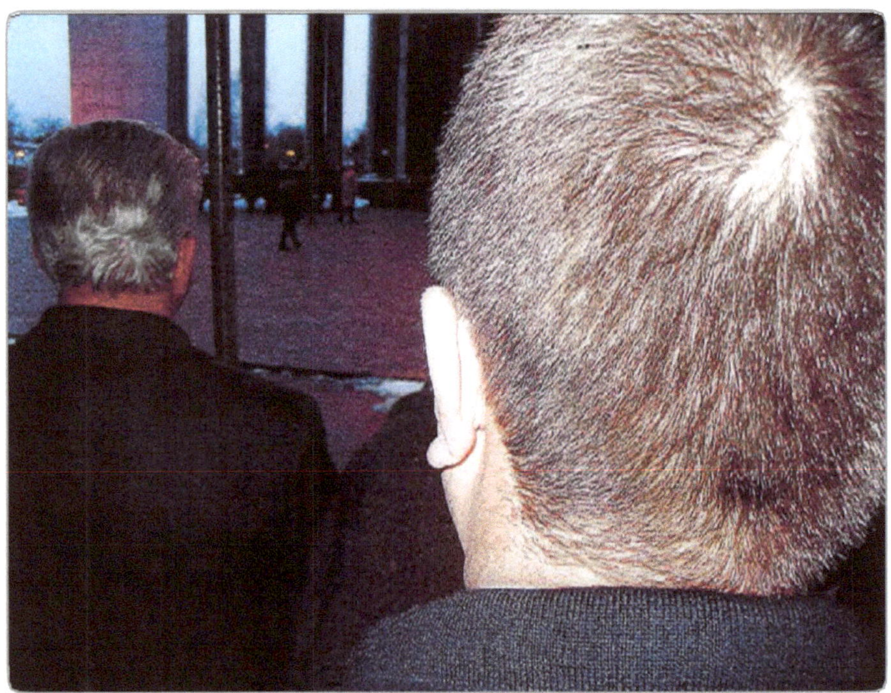

He walks up to the Memorial itself preparatory to laying a wreath in
homage to all those who fought, and died on Belgian soil.

He lays the wreath.

Outside the Hotel de Ville (City Hall) of Bastogne. The people are beginning to gather to take part, and to view the ceremony of Nutes. The area is decorated for Christmas season. A snow shower is in progress.

Everyone is waiting for the arrival of the King.

His Royal Majesty the King of Belgium.

His Majesty begins shaking his hands with the VBOB Vets gathered to meet, and greet him, exchange a few words, and receive a decoration from him. First in line to receive the honors was Bill Leopold.

Bill Leopold showing me that he got the decoration.

The King comes back to Bill to ask him about his family tree since
both share the same name, namely Leopold.

Continuation of what was happening in #192 above.

However, the King is now joined by the American Ambassador to Belgium, the gray headed man in the blue striped suit.

The talk goes on!

Heading my way, but the King pays his respect to the Nurses who served with us.

The King and the US Ambassador to Belgium continuing their conversation with the
Army Nurses.

VETERANS OF THE
BATTLE OF THE BULGE

VETERANS OF THE
BATTLE OF THE BULGE

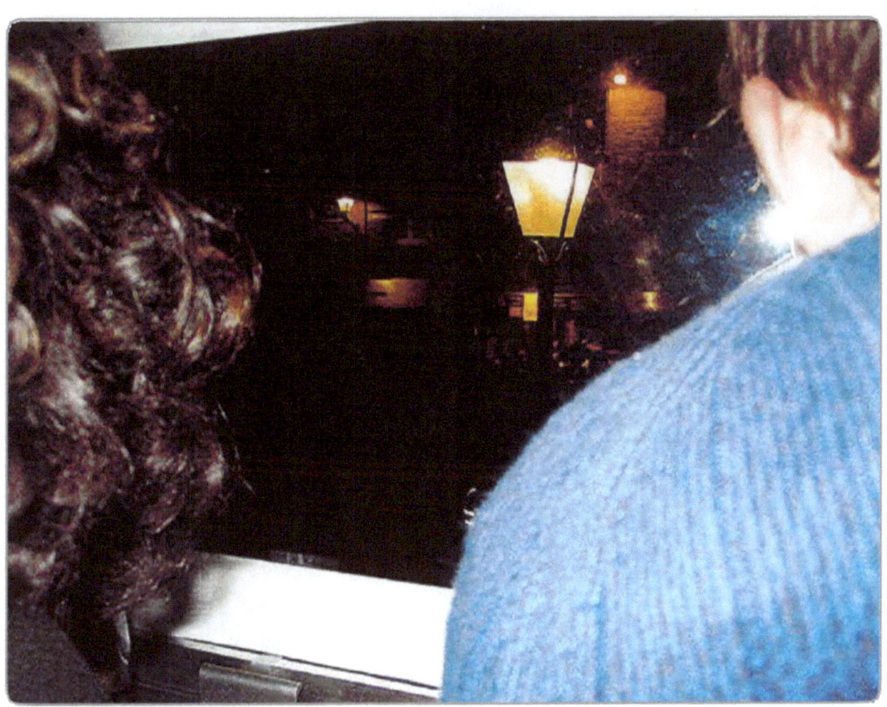

A random shot through a window in an attempt to capture some of the Nuts Celebration going on outside the City Hall.

Showing the award that I just received.

Coz who was not familiar with the camera that I was using took two pictures just to make sure.

Long range view of King of Belgium greeting the veterans.

Stained glass windows that arch up behind the main altar in the Cathedral of Our-Lady
RC Church in Luxembourg City.

Showing of the metals we got.

I took this shot to capture the Lady with the TV camera in the background. She conducted a 20 minute interview of me during the USO night held in Luxembourg. She told me the interview would appear in an armed services documentary on the Pentagon Station. She promised to send me a DVD of the interview.

Milly Thill who shepherd us around Luxembourg City, talking with
Helen Patton, granddaughter of General Patton.

Up front, and personal with Patoon's granddaughter.

The back of the Cathedral showing the great organ.

Vets engage Helen Patton in conversation.

A grand sweep of the main altar with the curved stain glass windows as a backdrop.

A courtesy shot to two vets, one old and one young.

Another view of the organ with a balconied area for the choir on each side.

A closer view to show the stained glass windows behind the organ pipes.

Gathered together in a plaza outside the church for a quick walking tour through the alleys, and narrow streets of the old city of Luxembourg. Milly Thill is our guide. The view is of buildings built to fortify the city by previous Dukes. It was very cold!!! Brrrrrrr....!

During the Nazi occupation this building was used by the Gestapo. It is but a short walk from the Duke's palace. There is a full blown enlargement of this building erected beside it. It shows a line of Lux people waiting to enter Gestapo Headquarters.

The building with twin guard houses is the Duke's palace. During the occupation the guards were Nazi soldiers with machine pistols.

The rear gate to the palace.

The old city of Luxembourg has many alleys, and narrow streets. This one winds
its way through what once was a fortified portion of an old castle.

The Alzette River winding through the old city.

Ramparts of old forts line both sides of the riverbank.

St. Joseph's RC Church, and seminary on the right bank.
More of the ramparts of an old fort on the left bank.

Luxembourgers call this place Christmas City. It contains over a hundred booths where you can buy almost anything. We found a McDonald's amongst the many eating places that are there. It was great getting to taste a bit of home once again.

...he Reception area of the Aventre Park Hotel in Luxembourg City where we were staying. Jack Dederer, and cronies are waiting to sit down, and eat the farewell dinner of the tour.

Frank Maresca

The dinner in progress.

Saying farewell.

More of the same.

Etc., Etc., Etc.

Looking over extra photos to take home.

And the chewing of food, the tingling of glasses, the clanging of silverware, and the unending chatter helped to drown out the approaching moments that the tour is over! Those taking commercial flights home ate before we Airbus folk. They didn't leave much for us to eat too!

The Airbus gang scrounging for the leftovers.

Coz and others pondering flight connection times with our flight schedule.

Brussels Airport where we landed about 14 days ago. That's the Airbus being fueled, and spruced up for our trip back. Yours truly posing on a spot overlooking the Airbus.

Boarding the Airbus for home.

Telefoto shot of the Airbus.

Underway! The Airbus was big with lots of room to stretch out or walk around. Provided a great ride both ways!

Another view of the roominess of this plane!

To avoid a bad turbulent storm, our captain flew around it thereby
necessitating a stop at Gander, Newfoundland to refuel.

The reception area at Gander. I make a P run, and call home.

Waiting for our luggage at Andrews Air Force Base.

Waiting at the conveyors for luggage.

The conveyors for picking up luggage.

The entrance to the Marriott Hotel where I joined the Airbus group. I was tired to make the 4 hours ride home, especially at night.

My last shot on my Compact card. I spent it on photoing the Hotel's garage where my faithful car awaited me for the trip to Effort, PA.

Someone once said that all things must come to an end. This isn't heaven where everything lasts forever.

The time frame of December 6th to the 21st embraced a brief moment in the collective lives of VBOB Veterans. Yet, it gave each one a chance to go back, not in time, but in memory, and in reality, to where searing experiences, sufferings, losses, pains, and sacrifices were made when they were but 18 or 19 years of age.

It is true that one can't go back to where it all began from where one is now, and find it as it was then. Nevertheless, for each man who was there; went through hell on earth for a brief moment, what he personally experienced, and what he remembers, made up for what he may not have found during the tour.

In spite of all this, each one was glad that he went back. That governments of Belgium, and Luxembourg, the VBOB organization, its appointed members who served as Coordinator (Earle Hart), his able assistants (Christian D'Haese, Micke Snoeckx, John Bowen), the staffs of organizations affiliated with the Bulge Commemoration, made it possible for all to have a wonderful time; to experience friendships lost but regained; faded memories brightened, and sharpened once again.

We can't express in words what surged through us during the days as the trip unfolded. Words were blocked by too many emotions. However, one of us did sum it up for all of us.

Jack Dederer said "I wouldn't have missed this trip for the world" And if I can add my two cents: in the words of the cowardly lion in the Wizard of Oz... Ain't that the truth"